Asterix

Annual

WORLD & WHITMAN

Published in Great Britain by World Distributors (Manchester) Limited.
A Pentos Company. P.O. Box 111, 12 Lever Street, Manchester M60 1TS.
Printed in Belgium.   SBN 7235 6569 4

Julius Caesar

Aquarium, Laudanum and Compendium which surround the village.

Julius Caesar, for his part, can't quite believe that all that stands between him and the total conquest of Gaul is a collection of so-called barbarians . . . .

Asterix is one of them. He is a shrewd, brave and wiry little warrior who is entrusted with all the dangerous missions that the villagers sometimes have to undertake. He may look small, and not very strong, but he's a match for any Roman, as many of the legionaries will testify. And it's not *just* because of the secret magic potion brewed up for him by the village druid, which makes him invincible, for Asterix uses cunning, too.

The GAULS...
and the ROMANS

The year is 50BC, and the great Roman armies have swept across most of Europe, conquering country after country. Julius Caesar, a clever tactician and a brilliant leader, was an ambitious man, and had already conquered most of Gaul, or France as we now know it. But he also wanted to conquer the tribes living in the more northern parts of Europe, too: namely, the rest of Gaul, then Britain and Germania (Germany). He took every chance to conquer new lands; he aimed, eventually, to be the sole master of the entire— and huge—Roman Empire.

Some tribes of Gauls were willing to become part of that great empire, and others, though resistant, were no match for the disciplined and highly organized Roman armies. Soon Caesar had conquered all of Gaul...

...All, that is, apart from one small village of Gauls on the northern coast of Armorica (now Brittany). The indomitable Gauls of that village are determined that they will *not* live under the Romans, Julius Caesar or no Julius Caesar, and they make life very hard for the Roman legionaries who garrison the fortified camps of Totorum,

Asterix

Cacofonix

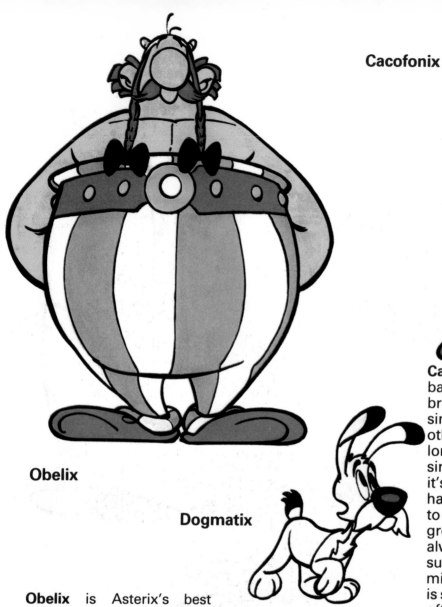

Obelix

Dogmatix

Cacofonix is the village bard. He thinks he's a brilliant musician and singer; the villagers think otherwise. All is well just so long as he doesn't start singing; as soon as he does, it's not. In fact, Cacofonix has to be bound and gagged to prevent him singing at the great banquets that are always held to celebrate the successful completion of a mission or battle. His music is so bad that the Gauls have often used it as a weapon against the Romans . . . .

Obelix is Asterix's best friend, more brawn than brain, but a very kindly Gaul. He makes his living quarrying huge stone monuments (menhirs) from the mountainsides. In fact, it is said that Stonehenge is the result of a few lessons that Obelix gave to the Britons when he was in their country. His two great loves are eating wild boar, and his little dog, **Dogmatix,** who he takes everywhere with him, even smuggling him along on dangerous adventures. Dogmatix is a kind of village mascot, and will have a go at anything—even Roman soldiers.

Getafix is the respected village druid, and the only one who knows the secret recipe for the magic potion. The potion makes anyone who drinks it immensely strong, though it does wear off after a time. (Obelix, incidentally, fell into a vat of magic potion when he was a baby, and it had a permanent effect on him, so he doesn't get—or need— any now). Even chiefs don't take important decisions without first consulting the village druid, so Getafix is a very important person indeed.

Getafix

Fulliautomatix is the village blacksmith, and a huge Gaul. He is so strong that he forges weapons with his bare hands!

Vitalstatistix

Vitalstatistix is the village chief, a brave and fearless warrior. The only person he is even *slightly* afraid of is his wife, **Impedimenta,** who is always urging her husband to live in the style of her rather grand relatives who live in Lutetia (Paris). Vitalstatistix is carried around on a great shield as a mark of his position and the great respect in which he is held. Due to his very *vital* statistics the 'honour' of carrying him around is thought a rather dubious one by some of the villagers!

Fulliautomatix

Unhygienix

Impedimenta

Unhygienix and his wife **Bacteria** are the fishmongers in the village. Though they live close to the sea, Unhygienix prefers to have his fish sent from Lutetia (Paris).

All together, the villagers would be quite happy to live the simple life that they like so much—lots of good food and drink, with a good fight now and then—but Julius Caesar and his armies just won't let them.

Asterix
at the
OLYMPIC GAMES

In normal times the greatest place of interest in Greece is the Acropolis . . .

. . .but at the time of the Olympic Games all eyes are fixed on Olympia. Our Gallic friends, the heroes of this story, are passing through Athens on their way to the Olympic Games.

The athletes are already hard at their training when our friends arrive.

"Are you all athletes?" ask the two cashiers, shocked. To their relief they hear that only Asterix and Obelix are taking part in the Games. To the dismay of the Gauls, only the two athletes and their trainer, together with their luggage and food, are allowed into the Olympic village.

While the other athletes train for many hours a day, our Gallic friends lead a quiet life. What's the point of training? Getafix has brought enough of the magic potion with him to ensure that Asterix isn't beaten.

Obelix fell into the potion as a child, so he is invincible. It was a pity that these facts had been brought to the attention of the Olympic committee. Our Gauls receive a strict warning.

The Olympic voice of authority has left our friends completely at a loss. Without their magic potion they don't stand a chance against all the athletes. All the Greeks and Romans taking part in the Games are naturally overjoyed. But Obelix doesn't understand the world any more; just because he fell into the magic potion pot as a child, he is not allowed to take part in the Olympic Games. It's just not fair, he thinks.

Asterix, Obelix and Getafix, their trainer, find their friends at their favourite pastime—holding a great banquet. The news the two athletes and their trainer bring is so alarming that they all stop eating. Vitalstatistix, their chief, is the first to comment.

"This is what we'll do," he says. "Asterix will compete in the Games...and...may luck be on our side!"

Asterix has begun training hard but on the eve of the Games he feels that all is lost. Still, Asterix's strength might come from the magic potion, but his intelligence is all his own.

"It's a pity you're not allowed a sip of the magic potion before the competition," says Obelix, so loudly that the athletes standing nearby can hear. They all prick up their ears.

The races the following day are staggering. All the competitors overtake Asterix without the slightest difficulty. And what is even more amazing, all except Asterix reach the finishing post at exactly the same time.

"You are cheats!" cries Asterix. "So are you!" cry the four winners.

"There!" says Getafix, pleased with himself. "All the ones with blue tongues have drunk the magic potion. Our Asterix is the victor!"

"The same to you, aaaaaah!"

Long live Asterix!

Well done, Asterix! And you did it without the magic potion. You were the only honest one!

What? Has Asterix won?

In a certain sense, yes Obelix!

Asterix AND Obelix

It is the year 50BC. After prolonged fighting, the Gauls are finally defeated by the Romans. The whole of Gaul is occupied. The *whole* of Gaul? Not quite— one village has resisted the Roman attack.

Here are the two heroes of our story, brave little Asterix and his faithful friend Obelix. Obelix's attention sometimes wanders....

If Obelix were a weak person like you or I, then he would have simply bumped into the tree. But Obelix fell into Getafix's magic potion when he was a child, and the potion has given

him super-human powers for the rest of his life. The tree which Obelix bumps into falls with a loud crash. Unfortunately the poor druid, Getafix, falls with it, for that was the tree he had been cutting mistletoe from.

Obelix tries to defend himself. He is astounded that he is not forgiven immediately. I don't know what he means, shrugs Asterix. Neither do I, howls Dogmatix, Obelix's little dog.

It's not good enough, thinks Dogmatix, a woman only has to walk past, and he forgets his best friends. What has come over him all of a sudden? He was always so sensible.

He even forgets the wild boar until Asterix wakes him from his daydream . . .

Asterix begins to make his worries known to his friends. He runs to Getafix and tells him how strangely Obelix has been behaving just recently. "He bumps into trees, leaves the Romans alone...doesn't

eat..." Asterix stops in mid sentence, for Obelix is passing and hasn't even seen them. "Obelix, where are you going?" asks Asterix. "Mmmm?" stutters Obelix. "I am delivering a menhir!"

Getafix is a very wise old man with great experience. Suddenly he realises what is wrong with Obelix. He is in love. Why else would he be for ever running after the beautiful Panacea?

Panacea is charming! She stretches out her hand to Obelix. The poor chap is so astounded that he can only mumble incomprehensible words. Dogmatix is not at all impressed, he is jealous.

14

Panacea says goodbye. But Obelix is still standing with outstretched hand and gazes after her, completely bewitched. He is quite lost in the new feelings which have suddenly come over him.

Asterix and Getafix look away, but they can no longer control themselves. They burst out laughing and just cannot stop. And then Obelix finally wakes from his trance.

"What do you mean? What do you mean?" he asks, embarrassed. "My dear friend, you're in love!" grins Asterix. "Rubbish!" says Obelix, trying to defend himself. "I have no potion to cure that!" says Getafix, and he leaves.

"A present's a good idea!" says Obelix, surprised. "You know about so many things!" And, in a flash, he's back again, "What?" calls Asterix. "Is *that* what you're going to give her?" And then he bursts out laughing again . . .

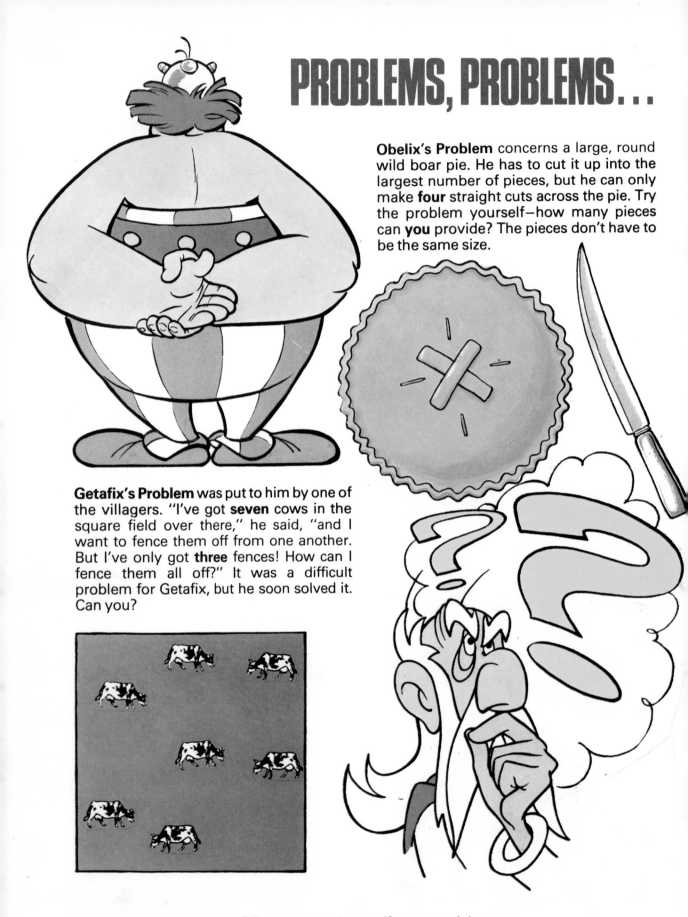

PROBLEMS, PROBLEMS...

Obelix's Problem concerns a large, round wild boar pie. He has to cut it up into the largest number of pieces, but he can only make **four** straight cuts across the pie. Try the problem yourself—how many pieces can **you** provide? The pieces don't have to be the same size.

Getafix's Problem was put to him by one of the villagers. "I've got **seven** cows in the square field over there," he said, "and I want to fence them off from one another. But I've only got **three** fences! How can I fence them all off?" It was a difficult problem for Getafix, but he soon solved it. Can you?

Did you solve the problems? Turn to page 62 to see if you were right.

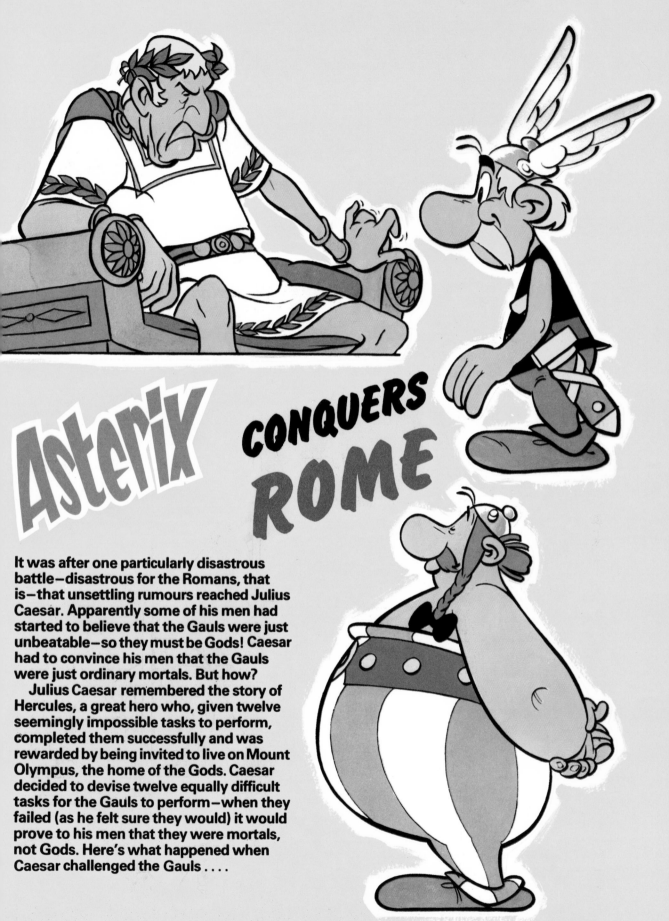

Asterix CONQUERS ROME

It was after one particularly disastrous battle—disastrous for the Romans, that is—that unsettling rumours reached Julius Caesar. Apparently some of his men had started to believe that the Gauls were just unbeatable—so they must be Gods! Caesar had to convince his men that the Gauls were just ordinary mortals. But how?

Julius Caesar remembered the story of Hercules, a great hero who, given twelve seemingly impossible tasks to perform, completed them successfully and was rewarded by being invited to live on Mount Olympus, the home of the Gods. Caesar decided to devise twelve equally difficult tasks for the Gauls to perform—when they failed (as he felt sure they would) it would prove to his men that they were mortals, not Gods. Here's what happened when Caesar challenged the Gauls . . . .

20

25

OBELIX IS NOT CUT OUT TO BE A TIGHTROPE WALKER...

...AND NOR IS ASTERIX SO THAT SOON...

EEEK!

OH, WELL, NEVER MIND, WE'LL HAVE TO GET THEM. COMING, ASTERIX?

WAIT A MINUTE...

YES, LET'S GET THEM!

HORRID CREATURE!!!

PIF! PAF!

NASTY INEDI- -BLE THINGS!

YOUR NEXT TASK IS TO CLIMB A MOUTAIN...

WELL, IT'LL MAKE A CHANGE FROM ABYSSES...

41

SOON AFTER...

WELL, HAVE YOU CARRIED OUT MY INSTRUCTIONS?

YES, O CAESAR. JUST FOR STARTERS, THOSE UNHAPPY GAULS WILL HAVE TO TACKLE OUR FIERCEST GLADIATORS. THE SURVIVORS, IF ANY, WILL BE THROWN TO THE WILD BEASTS! WE HAVE LIONS, TIGERS, PANTHERS, BEARS, EVEN ELEPHANTS... A GREAT PROGRAMME! THE AUDIENCE WILL BE WILD ABOUT IT!

ALL RIGHT... BRING ON THE GLADIATORS!

HURRAH!!!

LONG LIVE CAESAR!!!

HURRAH!!!

HURRY UP! I THINK IT'S OUR TURN NOW!

RIGHT, EVERYONE'S HAD HIS POTION!

COME ALONG, BOYS, AND KINDLY KEEP IN LINE. THERE ARE GOING TO BE CROWDS OF PEOPLE WATCHING US, SO LET'S SHOW A BIT OF DIGNITY! I GO FIRST, AND THE REST OF YOU FOLLOW ME!

AND WHY DO YOU THINK YOU GO FIRST O CHIEF VITALSTATISTIX?

BECAUSE I'M THE CHIEF, THAT'S WHY!

IT'S OUR RIGHT TO GO FIRST. WE'VE BEEN DOING ALL THE WORK.

WELL THEN, IT'S OUR TURN FOR A BIT OF FUN!

THAT'S RIGHT! I BACK FULLIAUTOMATIX! SOME PEOPLE GET ALL THE LUCK.

IN THE BEST CIRCLES THEY LET WOMEN GO FIRST!

WOMEN AND CHI- -DREN FIRST!

I'M THE OLDEST INHABITANT! IT'S MY RIGHT TO GO FIRST!

TARAAAA TARAHHHH!!!

FORCE THE GAULS INTO THE ARENA!

WHAT'S GOING ON?!!!

NO IDEA, O CAESAR!

TARAA!

LEAVE THEM TO ME! LEAVE THEM TO ME!

NO, WE WON'T! NO FEAR! WHY SHOULD WE?

Something Fishy....

Unhygienix and his wife Bacteria have just had a fresh delivery of fish from Lutetia, but the labels on the fish boxes are unreadable; the letters are all jumbled up. Can you help Unhygienix and Bacteria by unscrambling the letters to find the names? Write your answers in the spaces provided, then turn to page 62 to check your answers.

1. IKEP
_____

2. MONLAS
_____

3. DOC
_____

4. EKAH
_____

5. PRAC
_____

6. NUTA
_____

7. DHODACK
_____

8. BUTIHAL
_____

and Asterix
VITALSTATISTIX

Peace reigns in the small Gallic village which we know so well. As always, its inhabitants are friendly and happy.

Vitalstatistix's birthday is always an event to be celebrated in style. All the villagers are pleased about it—they all enjoy a good feast!

Naturally there are all sorts of preparations to be made. First of all they have to decide what presents the chief is to receive this year. This is a problem which all the villagers will have to consider very seriously.

At the end of the discussion they are all agreed; each man will give the chief whatever he himself considers particularly valuable. Obelix has decided on a menhir—as every year; Asterix a shield—as every year—and so on...

In Vitalstatistix's house there are also problems. The chief makes the same speech every year on his birthday, but nevertheless he always prepares it with great care. He practises each gesture carefully....

The storing of presents is really a great problem. Impedimenta has to make room for them all. The week's dusting alone is a mammoth task!

"If only these clumsy menhirs were lovely ornaments for our home!" scolds Impedimenta. "But no, they just take up space and create dust. And it's exactly the same with the swords and the fish and the shields...."

47

Vitalstatistix does not share his wife's opinion. In his view it doesn't matter what sort of presents he receives. The fact that he is receiving presents is enough for him.

The villagers are quiet, partly out of joy at their chief's gratitude and partly for other reasons. Obelix is thinking of the juicy wild boar he will be eating that evening; Asterix is thinking of hearty toasts!

The shield-bearers have made a grave mistake! They thought their chief's words about bowing applied to them too! Hardly surprising that Vitalstatistix is raging! Whenever they carry him through a door they *forget* to bow.

And that isn't too pleasant for Vitalstatistix's head! Even in 50BC there were unfortunate misunderstandings between people. "May the sky fall upon your head!" cries the chief.

That evening the great banquet takes place. Under the starry sky (which doesn't fall upon *anyone's* head) the Gauls are assembled for their traditional feast.

THE BIRTHDAY FEAST

I am lost for words, my friends, on the occasion of this wonderful surprise...

The following morning...

"We still have a problem," reflects Getafix. "What are we to give the chief for his *next* birthday?" "No problem," says Obelix. "I shall give him a menhir and...."

That was a feast to remember! I haven't tasted such fine wild boar in a long time!

Obelix, how would you like a hearty breakfast to celebrate the morning after?

WHAT'S HAPPENING HERE?

Fill in each area using the same colour as its dot to find out what's happening.

CACOFONIX'S QUIZ

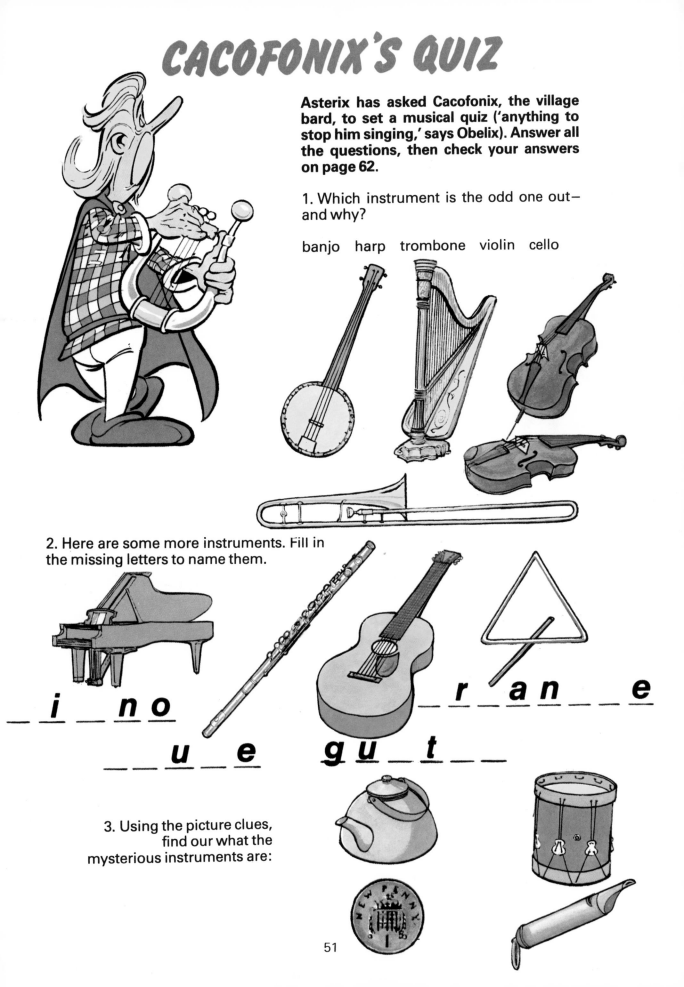

Asterix has asked Cacofonix, the village bard, to set a musical quiz ('anything to stop him singing,' says Obelix). Answer all the questions, then check your answers on page 62.

1. Which instrument is the odd one out—and why?

banjo   harp   trombone   violin   cello

2. Here are some more instruments. Fill in the missing letters to name them.

_ _ i _ n o

_ _ _ u _ e

g u _ t _ _

r _ a n _ e

3. Using the picture clues, find our what the mysterious instruments are:

51

and the ROMANS

In the little village of our great Gallic heroes Getafix the druid is making final prepatations for his journey into the Karnute Forest. Each year the Gallic druids meet in the forest to exchange their secret potions and experiences, and also to elect the Druid of the Year.

"I'll come with you, Getafix," offers Asterix, "to make sure you get to the Karnute Forest safely!" Obelix wants to come, too. And Cacofonix, the village bard? Oh, no, certainly not . . . .

After safely escorting Getafix, Asterix and Obelix take a stroll in the forest. They are not allowed to go into the Karnute Forest; that is forbidden to non-druids. But what's this?

While the druids are assembling in the Karnute Forest, Asterix and Obelix are walking nearby. It passes the time, for the druid meeting takes longer and longer every year.

Terrific! Obelix is already happily anticipating a fight. That's how things are with the Romans since they occupied Gaul; they interfere in everything. Even in things which don't concern them!

It so happens that these Roman soldiers know nothing of the magic potion which makes our Gallic friends invincible. These soldiers are quite unsuspecting.

Once again we can see what happens when hasty conclusions are drawn! One Gothic helmet does not necessarily mean a whole band of Goths! Asterix is shocked at their extreme stupidity, although he has never thought much of the Romans.

Stupidity has overcome both Romans. And if nothing is to be gained by politeness, then other means of communication must be tried! And our two Gallic friends are specialists in communication with the Romans, that's for sure!

Obelix is really in his element now! As a child, he fell into the magic potion which Getafix brews up. It is a potion which gives super-human powers.

Whilst Asterix must take regular sips for strength, the potion's effects never wear off on Obelix. The fight between the Gauls and the Romans is short . . . .

Unfortunately the Gothic helmet is lost in the fearsome battle. So Asterix and Obelix make their way back to the Karnute Forest where their friend Getafix is awaiting them. He has been nominated Druid of the Year. ''Well done!'' cries Asterix.

What a welcome they get when they reach the village . . .

And then . . .ho ho ho . . . Dekurion said, "That was definitely those Goths!" Ha! Ha! Ha!

Give him another wild boar, quickly or he'll be telling it all over again!

Poor Cacofonix! He only wanted to sing a song!

A huge feast had been arranged for the two heroes. They eat, drink and laugh far into the night, and recount the whole adventure in great detail.

END

55

Where are my Porters?

Vitalstatistix and his porters have become separated out in the woods. Vitalstatistix is anxious to get home because if he's late his wife, Impedimenta, will be very angry with him, so he goes chasing off along the narrow paths to find them. Go along with him and try to guide him along the right paths until he reaches his porters.

WHO'S HIDING?

There is a Gaul hiding on this page. To find out who it is, fill in each area of the picture using the same colour as its dot.

57

Asterix THE GAUL

Once again it is time to brew up the magic potion, a potion which gives the Gauls strength and makes them invincible. Getafix, the druid, needs fresh mistletoe from the forest for the potion. Asterix is bored.

He wants to go with Getafix. "Better stay here and guard the village," says Getafix. Soon he is walking happily through the forest, humming to himself. "CRASH!" The druid disappears down a man-trap.

Roman soldiers suddenly appear from the bushes. And Getafix, despite his loud protests, is tied up and taken to the Roman camp. The Romans want him to tell them the secret of the magic potion.

In spite of everything, the Romans are having little success interrogating the druid. They try threats, torture (which he doesn't feel anyway) and even promises, but nothing will persuade him to reveal his secret.

Asterix becomes anxious when it gets even later and there's still no sign of the druid. "Be careful—it's ages since you had a draught of the magic potion," warns his friend Obelix, who is just passing by with a menhir.

But nothing will deter Asterix. Finally he meets a man driving a cart on the road to Rome. "Have you seen a druid, by any chance?" asks Asterix, as he climbs up on to the seat beside him.

"I have seen one, but he was in a net and the legionaries were carrying him to Aquarium. Aquarium is where the legionaries are holding camp." Just outside Aquarium Asterix hides under the hay.

That's where he'll be! But Asterix stays in the hay until it gets dark. Then he begins his search for Getafix. He creeps through the camp until he comes across a tent closely guarded by two soldiers.

"Do you mind, gentlemen?" says Asterix. "I just want to go and free my friend Getafix." And with that he strolls into the tent. Getafix is lying tied to a table and looks up at Asterix anxiously.

Meanwhile, both guards have announced the arrival of the enemy Gaul. At first, Asterix intends to fight bravely against the superior strength of the Romans but then he has a really strange idea. He gives himself up!

Asterix willingly submits to the torture. The Roman torturer is amazed at the Gaul's lack of courage. "But I've only just begun," he says disappointedly.

Finally Getafix declares that he will brew up the Romans a cauldron of the magic potion. The general and his soldiers stand round the cauldron expectantly. The general, Gaius Bonus, can hardly wait.

The potion is hardly ready when he snatches the spoon from Getafix and takes a huge gulp. But he feels no strength growing in him; the only thing that starts to grow is his beard!

Asterix and Getafix make themselves scarce in the general confusion. They are still laughing out loud. And what has become of the general, Gaius Bonus? Well, his beard is growing still!

Asterix and Getafix are howling with laughter. Hopefully the Romans have at last learned that a Gaul is not to be forced into anything! "Suits you, that beard!" says Asterix and bursts out laughing again.

ANSWERS

PROBLEMS, PROBLEMS...

Obelix's Problem: He provided eleven pieces of wild boar pie by making four cuts like this:

Getafix's Problem: This is how he fenced off the seven cows using only three fences:

SOMETHING FISHY .

1. Pike; 2. Salmon; 3. Cod; 4. Hake; 5. Carp; 6. Tuna; 7. Haddock; 8. Halibut.

CACOFONIX'S QUIZ

1. The trombone is the odd one out; all the others are stringed instruments; 2. Piano, flute, guitar and triangle; 3. Kettle-drum and penny-whistle.